WYLDE

Arizona Vengeance

Sawyer Bennett

Find Sawyer on the web!
sawyerbennett.com
www.twitter.com/bennettbooks
www.facebook.com/bennettbooks

TABLE OF CONTENTS

CHAPTER 1

Wylde

I LOVE LIVING in downtown Phoenix. My condo is on the fringe of the social scene, which is filled with trendy cafes, fine dining, and upscale shopping. At night, I merely have to step out of my building and walk one block west to be in the thick of it all. Five blocks south, and I'm at the arena where the Vengeance plays. My truck mostly stays parked in the underground garage unless I need to use it to drive to the airport for away games, but I'll often just Uber it.

I've always preferred city living, and I lived in downtown Dallas when I played hockey for the Mustangs before being traded to the Arizona Vengeance. It's a single man's playground, the city life, and I wouldn't trade it for one of those houses in the burbs that a lot of my teammates choose as their choice destination for fine living.

I ignore the elevator on the fourth floor of my building, choosing to take the stairs instead. For fuck's sake, I'm a professional athlete... I should be able to handle four flights of stairs coming and going.

When I step out into the June morning, it still takes me a moment to get past the startling dry heat. It seems like I'd be used to it since I've lived the last several years in the southwest between Dallas and Phoenix, but this New Englander still has a tough time living without humidity.

Regardless, today is the day I'd chosen to get back into the swing of things with my workouts and I can't let a little fire in the lungs before I even start my run stop me.

It was just ten days ago that my team, the Arizona Vengeance, won the Cup championship over the defending champions, the Carolina Cold Fury. It's been ten days of being lazy, eating bad food, and drinking lots of beer. I've been going out with my single buds on the team almost every night, getting drunk and heading home with a different puck bunny.

But fuck, I can only take so much of that type of hedonism. Like I said, I'm a professional athlete and with that comes a certain way of living.

For my entire hockey-playing life—starting before I was a teen—I'd taken my training seriously. I'd been told by coaches early on I had raw talent, but part of developing that was in conditioning my body. That meant good nutrition, workouts, and maintaining a winning attitude at all times, even in the off-season.

That's where we are now... the glorious off-season of summer, but that doesn't mean I don't have to work.

Starting today, it's back on. Training camp is only three short months away, and the pressure for us to perform at the same or better standards is immense. On top of that, my contract expires at the end of next season, and I'll be damned if I'm going to operate at anything less than one hundred percent.

So today, I start back running and I usually average at least twenty miles a week, broken into four or five morning runs.

Many of my defense peers aren't into running, focusing instead on strength training and muscle endurance. Those are important, too, but I've always loved running for some reason. I'm easily able to let my head go into a subspace, and it's quite meditative for me. On top of that, it burns a lot of calories. It means I can eat more, which is a bonus given how much I love food.

I take a moment on the sidewalk to do some dynamic stretching—heel-to-toe stretches, hamstring curls, and leg kicks. I do two sets, walking up and down my condo's block, oblivious to the people who do double-takes when they recognize me.

For the most part, that doesn't happen. Yes, I'm a

well-known player for the Arizona Vengeance, a first-line defenseman, but the entire city isn't into hockey. More often than not, I'm able to go places without being recognized, but that's also dependent on where I go. Sports bars, I'm bound to get approached for autographs. The grocery store, less likely, particularly since I like to go early on Sunday mornings when it's practically dead.

Legs fully stretched, I start off in a slow jog heading east and after the first quarter-mile, I pick up the pace. My earbuds are cranked, and DJ Khalil elevates me to run faster.

My mind wanders, trying to figure out my summer. I haven't given it a lot of thought as I'm more of an impulsive, do-things-when-I-feel-like-it kind of guy. I know I should plan a trip home to New Hampshire to see my mom, but the thought of it starts to depress and demotivate me, so I put it out of my head. We don't have the best relationship and any trips home are made from a sense of obligation, not because I actually get joy from our reunions.

That may seem harsh, but she'd say the same damn thing.

Normally, I'd plan a vacation on a sunny beach somewhere but in a few weeks, I'll be headed to the U.S. Virgin Islands to attend Brooke and Bishop's wedding. The entire team is going for a week to participate in a continued celebration of the Cup win in addition to their nuptials. It's going to be just one long party, and I'm looking forward to it.

Maybe I could head to Wyoming for a few days of fishing, something I got into over the last few years and really enjoy.

Or maybe I should go bum around Europe for a bit. I have several teammates who would be up for just such an adventure.

Regardless, anything I decide will have to wait until after Bishop and Brooke's wedding during the first week of July because my weekends are already accounted for until then.

Up ahead, I see they're doing some sidewalk construction on my normal route. At the next light, I decide to turn left, jogging in place while I wait for the light to change. As other mid-morning strollers casually jaunt over the crosswalk, I take off running again. Rush hour is over and most people are at their places of work, but I still have to weave in and out of other pedestrians.

This is a street I haven't been on. I pass a coffee shop, a small drugstore, and what looks like a bookshop.

I glance in the window of the latter, my gaze landing on an incredibly gorgeous woman behind the cash register. It's really just a glimpse as I run by, but her auburn-colored hair gathered in a messy bun on top of her head and the most stunning pair of eyes shining from under a pair of rectangular, black-framed glasses catch my attention.

Now, glasses aren't normally my thing on a woman, but, in this instance, they work. I can't tell if her eyes are green or blue, but they're light-colored, in stark contrast against her fiery hair with tendrils escaping her updo and framing her pretty face.

And just as quickly as I spot her, she's gone because I'm past the bookstore and reaching the end of the block.

To return to my route, I should cut right and head uptown, but I can't shake that tiny glimpse of gorgeousness I just witnessed, so I decide to take another peek at the woman. I kick up my pace. Rather than turn around and go back, I decide to circle the block to get my paces in.

When I reach the bookstore and slow my pace to get a better look at the woman, disappointment sets in because she's no longer behind the register. I can't spot her anywhere. Granted, there's a lot going on inside the shop. It's more than just a bookstore as in addition to rows of books, there are tables and free-standing shelves that host a variety of knickknacks for sale. It looks cozy, interesting, and crowded at the same time, but there's no beautiful redhead.

And once again, the bookstore is behind me—the opportunity she represented now firmly in my rearview mirror.

I get to the end of the block, determined to turn right and get back on route. For some reason, though, I don't enter the crosswalk when the light turns green. Jogging in place, I peek over my shoulder at the bookstore, weighing my options.

"Fuck it," I mutter, pivoting and heading back that way.

Slowing to a walk a good ten yards from the door, I take deep breaths to get my heart rate into a normal range and cut the sound from my iPhone strapped onto my bicep. My breathing evens out quickly because, despite the ten days of gluttony and debauchery, I'm still in great shape. I reach an arm up, wipe my sweaty brow on my sleeve, and take one last deep breath.

Pushing open the door to the bookstore, I note the name painted in gold letters—*Clarke's Corner*. A tinkling bell announces my arrival, and a husky voice calls out from somewhere behind the bookshelves.

"Be there in a moment."

"Take your time," I reply loud enough to carry, then proceed to browse around.

It's an incredibly cute place. All the furniture, including the four long rows of bookshelves that are jam-packed with paperbacks and hardcover editions, are painted in a glossy white. The walls are done in a pale blue, covered with paintings by what look to be local

sheepish but hopefully charming smile. "Not the best shopper."

The woman moves over to a wall unit that houses a few interesting pieces of pottery, then chooses a vase the color of burnt cinnamon with dark yellow swirling through it. "How about something like this?"

Taking it from her, I pretend to study it thoughtfully before I shake my head. "I don't think this is to their taste."

In truth, it very well could be. I'm not good at stuff like this, but if I accept the first thing she shows me, then the conversation is over and I'll have to leave.

She next shows me a pair of brass candlesticks. "Too formal," I say.

A porcelain picture frame. "Too feminine."

A music box. "Also too feminine."

Next up is a fancy wine opener. Well, that's actually a really good gift. Reluctantly, I nod with a smile. "It's perfect."

"Awesome," she replies, moving past me to get to the register. She smells of vanilla with an undertone of what might be oranges. It's pretty, and I can't quite remember the last time a woman's fragrance appealed to me.

"Would you like me to gift wrap this?" she asks.

"That would be awesome," I reply, because anything that will give me the opening I need to ask her out is all right with me.

I am most definitely asking her out.

I mean, she's hot, but she has this nerdy quality going on with the glasses and innocent fragrance. Her clothes are slightly baggy, not the form-fitting, bare-all concoctions most women I hook up with wear.

She's like a breath of fresh air and this perplexes me, because I've never been overly attracted to her type before.

"So how long have you been working here?" I ask genially as she reaches under a cabinet behind the register to pull out a long bin with wrapping paper in it.

"I own the place," she replies without looking up. In her tone, there's amusement I would never even consider she was the owner, along with pride in herself that she owns this place.

"Wow," I reply, surprised and impressed. I turn around, taking in the store once more. She must be doing okay since this is a high-rent commercial district of Phoenix.

"Opened it about six months ago," she replies, rummaging through the bin. "Lifelong dream and all."

"Good for you." I lean on the checkout counter, watching her with appreciation while her back is turned. "So, I take it you're the 'Clarke' of 'Clarke's Corner'?"

Without warning, she glances over her shoulder and I manage to tear my eyes off her ass just in time. "That's me. Clarke Webber."

"Aaron Wylde," I reply in turn. I watch carefully to see if there's a glimmer of recognition, since I *am* a famous hockey player, after all. But she didn't seem to recognize my face when I walked in, or, if she did, she played it super cool.

Now, she just gives me a polite nod and murmurs, "Nice to meet you."

Yeah… she has no clue who I am, which means she's not a hockey fan. It isn't all that surprising. While the Vengeance coming to Phoenix last year generated immense buzz and excitement, not everyone is a fan. I saw a recent article that said TV viewership for the final Cup championship game was at 2.9 million. Contrasted to the 19.3 million people who watched the *Game of Thrones* finale, it's obvious professional hockey is a niche.

Clarke jolts me from my thoughts by turning to face me.

"Is this a formal wedding or something a bit more casual?" She holds up two different rolls of paper. I'm assuming one is fancy and the other isn't, but fuck if I can tell the difference.

"It's going to be an outdoor wedding, so I'd say maybe casual."

"Got it," she replies, attention returning to the wine opener. As she works at removing the price tag and wrapping it, I prattle on, which is weird for me. "It's kind of a spontaneous type thing. The couple is engaged, and they were going to do something bigger, but they had an accidental pregnancy, and decided to just go for it."

"Oh, good for them," she intones, and I can feel the smile in her words. "And, honestly, if they already have a wine opener—and chances are they do—it's always good to have a backup."

With the package wrapped, she starts to ring up the purchase. A surge of panic hits me when I realize that, once this exchange is complete, I'll be expected to walk out that door with a wrapped wine opener under my arm—which I don't need—and this gorgeous woman but a memory.

I struggle to think of *anything* to get our conversation where I need it so I can make a move. Ask her out and arrange something.

Fuck, this is hard.

I suppose it comes with the territory of being nothing but a playboy who prefers to hop from bed to bed. Also, it's a bit of an issue that I often rely on my looks or fame to get me where I'm going. Most of my hookups happen after games or in bars where literally dozens of puck bunnies throw themselves at me, and it's just a matter of choosing the one I'm most attracted to.

"What kind of books do you sell?" I blurt out.

Allen?

Aaron?

My eyes do a quick rake over his body. He's clearly what I'd peg as a part-time jock. He's wearing high-end athletic gear for his run. His watch is expensive-looking, which means he makes a good living—maybe a financial advisor? One of those guys who likes to stay in shape, so he looks good in his three-piece suit. I bet he's a member of an exclusive country club where he golfs five days a week and probably plays flag football on the side.

I give him a polite smile, because I want to roll my eyes at anyone who says they don't have time to read. If a person loves books the way I do, they'll find time to read. If they don't read, it's because they don't like to do it, which makes them something of a moron in my mind.

I mean... who doesn't like books? They give knowledge, elicit tears or laughter, and transport people to faraway places.

The dude is definitely weird.

"I'll go ahead and get this rung up—"

"Another wedding," he blurts out, then slaps his forehead as if he'd just remembered something critical to life on earth. "I actually have another wedding weekend after this, and I'll need a gift for that. And come to think of it, one in July, too. So I'll need two more."

"Oh… okay," I murmur, setting the wrapped wine opener on the counter and moving out from behind it. Dude is totally weird. "Let's see if we can find you something."

Fifteen minutes later, we have picked out a vase for one lucky couple and a table book of southwestern photography for the other. The man asks me to wrap those as well, which I do quickly before finally moving to ring him up.

"I know this might be coming out of left field," the man says with a bit of hesitation, "but would you have any interest in joining me as my date to the wedding this weekend? There's going to be a really great reception after with some awesome barbeque and a band."

I give him a smile, hoping it's appropriately polite and regretful. "That's very sweet of you to offer, but no thank you."

"Got a boyfriend?" he asks.

"No," I reply, then immediately curse myself. I should have said yes.

"Married?"

Damn you, truth. I shake my head. "No, but—"

"Then say yes," he pushes with oozing confidence, leaning on the counter and leveling an impish smile. I have to say, it's a really great smile, replete with dimples and everything.

"I'm sorry, Ervin—"

Annoyance flashes across his face. "Aaron."

"Aaron," I confirm, trying not to laugh. "But... um, well... you're not my type."

He blinks in surprise, and I can tell in this moment that no woman ever has told this man that.

"What exactly is your type?" he asks with a frown.

I really don't have one. I've dated a variety of men— a DJ, a sommelier, and a roof inspector just in the last few months. But something about this man has danger bells ringing faintly in the background—not from a safety perspective, but rather he just seems as if he has *complication* written all over him.

I always listen to my gut, so I pull forth somewhat of a lie, which I know will work based on what little he's revealed of himself. "I'm actually more into the brainy, nerdy types. You know... the ones who always have their noses buried in a book and can quote Proust on a whim."

He blinks, clearly not understanding a word I just said. Definitely a jock.

I seem to have shocked him into silence, as he doesn't say a word as I ring up his purchases. After I punch in the appropriate codes, I scan the tags and tally the total cost with tax. "That will be $179.32."

Aaron reaches into his side pocket, then pulls out a small clip securing some cash along with a single credit card. I slide it through the reader, then complete the transaction.

It's as I'm placing his gifts in a bag that he decides to take another stab at a date. "How about a little wager or competition? If I win, then you have to go to the wedding with me."

He's persistent, I'll give him that, and well... I have to admit he has my curiosity all riled up. I tilt my head. "Like what?"

"Well... I used to be a reader," he says quickly, now leaning on the counter again with both forearms resting there. His eyes are sparkling, filled with challenge. "You know... back in high school and such. How about you give me a well-known quote from your favorite classic and if I can guess what book it's from, you have to go to the wedding with me this weekend?"

I regard him, wondering if this is some type of trap. But no... he has no interest in books. I can tell by the fact he didn't bother perusing one shelf in my store that houses all kinds of amazing literature.

He's taking a shot in the dark, and no matter what quote I give him, he'll probably blurt out Melville's *Moby Dick* or something with a phallic reference.

"Okay," I muse, gaze traveling up to the ceiling where I ponder a moment all the wonderful classics I love. I dismiss a few he might take an easy guess at—*The Call of the Wild*, *To Kill A Mockingbird*, *Gulliver's*

Travels.

But one comes to mind… it seems fitting in this moment.

I give him a sly smile. "*The mark of the immature man is that he wants to die nobly for a cause, while the mark of the mature man is that he wants to live humbly for one.*"

Aaron's face is like a blank art canvas. He doesn't even try to search his memory as there's no furrowing of his brow or rubbing at his jaw in consternation.

I drop the receipt into his bag, push it across the counter, and try to keep all traces of smugness out of my expression.

"That's Salinger," Aaron says in a neutral tone. "*Catcher in the Rye*, I believe."

I'm surprised my jaw doesn't hit the counter it drops so low in disbelief, and I realize I've seriously misjudged this man. I completely characterized him as a rube, an unenlightened individual, and made that judgment based on his appearance and his current lack of time to read.

Or… he's playing me somehow.

I narrow my eyes with suspicion, which only amuses him.

"Want to go double or nothing?" he suggests. "I need a date to the wedding the weekend after this one, too."

It was a lucky guess. It had to be. *Catcher in the Rye* was too obvious. Anyone who graduated high school or college probably could have figured that out. I went far too easy on him.

"Deal," I reply, confident he'll never go two for two. I consider the possibilities again, deciding to focus on a piece of literature that tends to be favored by women over men.

Something romantic.

And pertinent.

I lift my chin. "*We all know him to be a proud, unpleasant sort of man; but this would be nothing if you really liked him.*"

I'm glad to see Aaron has a sense of humor and isn't offended, for he tips his head back and laughs before bringing his gaze back to mine. He shakes his head, as if to say, "Touché," and wags a finger.

A flush of triumph rolls through me, only to be quickly killed when he says, "*Pride and Prejudice.* Jane Austen."

"What in the absolute hell?" I mutter. "Are you cheating somehow?"

He holds his arms out, making a show of turning slowly. When facing me again, he asks, "With what? My secret quote book stashed somewhere on me?"

"You intentionally set me up," I accuse.

"No," he drawls, correcting my misstatement. "I

presented a challenge. You accepted it."

"I feel played," I mutter.

"Had you just asked if I were well-read first, you might have declined my challenge," he points out. "Not my fault my dad was an English professor and I'm pretty sure I can quote more classics than you—a bookstore owner—can."

Before I can even respond, the door to my shop flies open, the tinkling bells going berserk and the wooden frame encasing glass rattling hard when it hits a table. The woman who enters immediately ducks her head in embarrassment, offering me an apologetic shrug and mouthing the words, "Sorry."

That woman would be my best friend, Veronica. She's everything I'm not in the looks department. Long legs, busty, and with California golden-blonde hair. She's sporting a designer workout outfit, and she's carrying a specialty coffee from a shop down the street.

Aaron glances at her, but he doesn't linger, giving his attention right back. Pulling his phone off the strap around his bicep, he orders, "Give me your phone number."

Everything within me wants to deny him, but that's mostly self-loathing I'd misjudged him so much and let myself fall right into a date with a man I still have all kinds of danger alarms going off about.

With a grudge in my tone, I rattle off my number.

He types it into his phone, then immediately dials me. My phone is in my purse, under the counter behind me, but I ignore it. He's only calling to ensure I have his number, too. I'll input his contact info, then come up with some excuse to back out later. A simple text should suffice.

"I can see what's going on in that pretty head of yours," he teases, and my cheeks fire up. "And I get it... you could easily just text me to cancel after I leave, but that will be a matter for your conscience. I won fair and square, so I guess I'll just have to see how much honor you have."

A tiny growl wells in my throat that he would dare throw the gauntlet down. Integrity is important to me, so I know there's no way in hell I'll cancel now.

"You can text me your address, though," he says with a wink as he grabs the bag from the counter. "So I know where to pick you up on Saturday. Be ready around five PM."

I dart my glance behind him to Veronica. She's acting like she's only perusing my merchandise, but she's totally listening in.

Turning my attention to Aaron, I tilt my chin upward. "Not about to hand my address out to a perfect stranger. You can send me the address of where the wedding is taking place, and I'll meet you there."

"Fair enough," he replies as he turns away from me,

heading toward the door. Veronica is in his way, but he just gives her a polite nod and moves around her. She fans herself dramatically behind his back to indicate she thinks he's hot as hell, and I can't wait to tell her I'm sure he can see her reflection in the glass of the door.

When Aaron grabs the handle to pull it open, he looks back. "If you want to get to know me better before the wedding, give me a call. We can go out for a drink or dinner. Or we can just talk about classic literature if you'd like."

My face gets even hotter, another pointed reminder I'd totally misjudged him and we actually have something in common.

Stupid jock who isn't a jock, apparently.

The bells tinkle merrily as he pulls the door open and disappears onto the sidewalk. Veronica leans to the side, craning her neck so she can watch him walk down the street as long as possible. When he's out of her line of sight, she straightens and turns with an expression of wonder.

"Clarke Angelica Webber," she accuses as she saunters up to the counter. "You little minx. Flirting with the customers and scoring a date with an Adonis. Just look at you, girl."

"Shut up," I growl, not an ounce of teasing in my tone. I can get away with it because we've been friends for most of our lives, starting all the way back in preschool.

"No, you shut up," she replies automatically in an exaggeratedly snippy tone. Then she laughs, waving a hand. "Actually, don't shut up. Tell me everything from start to finish."

So I do, from the moment he walked in.

"Oh, damn," she murmurs in awe, snapping her fingers. "And he just threw out J.D. Salinger as if it were nothing. Wow."

"I should have sensed it was a trap," I grumble.

"Why are you so upset?" Veronica asks, taking a sip of her coffee before offering me a taste. I take the cup, lift it to my mouth, and smell cinnamon.

Delicious.

I swallow, keeping her coffee in my hand as I move around the counter. We move over to a pair of Victorian-styled chairs in the corner, which I'd set up for customers who might want to peruse a book for a bit. When she takes a seat, I do the same, lifting her coffee for another sip before handing it back to her.

"He's just not my type," I say, hoping she won't dig further.

But this is Veronica. She knows me inside and out, warts, weaknesses, and ugly anxieties. "You mean he's confident, gorgeous, and gregarious."

"I like confident men," I argue, but even I hear the lie in those words.

Legend Bay. It means Baden has to be in prime condition at all times, ready to step on the ice at a moment's notice and expected to play at a level equal to or greater than Legend. It's a huge responsibility for a backup goalie—the pressure to perform is immense. While Legend took the vast majority of games this season and was never injured—knock on wood—Baden guarded the net on several occasions and was quite remarkable earning a .927 save percentage by the end of the season. It meant our team was formidable because we had a goalie who could easily carry us through should something happen to Legend, which was a commodity many teams would kill for.

These are my new buds, the singles, who I hang with while my closest friends enjoy the harmony of monogamy and true love.

I can't help but snort, because while I'm happy for my friends, it's not something I really aspire to attain.

I mean… one day, sure. When I'm retired from the game, and I'm ready to settle down. Until then, I get all the willing pussy I could ever want, answer to no one, and have the best friends in the world. Who could want more than that?

Looking to my left, I ask Kane, "You finally all settled in?"

The poor dude had to make a move across the country right at the start of the playoffs just two months ago.

It has been non-stop practices, team meetings, travel, and games since. He'd been basically living out of boxes.

But now we've had a few weeks since the championship game for everyone to get settled into the off-season.

Kane nods. "Finally got everything unpacked, but I still have an entire room full of cardboard boxes I've got to take to the dump at some point."

Kane lives just a block from me in another condo unit downtown, so I offer, "Let me know when you want to do it, and I'll help. We can load it all up in the back of my truck."

"Or bring it to my house," Jim interjects. "We can burn that shit in the backyard while we drink beers."

"Pretty sure there's a perpetual burning ban in the southwest," Baden points out. "You'd get arrested."

Jim grins and shrugs. "Hey... what happens in the off-season, stays in the off-season."

"Tell that to Dominik." I give Jim a pointed look. "You'll find yourself on the fast track to play in the Siberian league."

While it's true our esteemed owner is equal parts generous and giving to his team, he also demands excellence on all fronts. Having his players arrested for any reason would not sit well with him.

Of course, I suppose it all worked out for Tacker. He got arrested for drunk driving, but Dominik made him jump through some pretty tall hoops to stay with the team, one of which was mandatory counseling.

Tacker's my best friend, head and shoulders above the rest. We played together in Dallas, and luckily, we reunited on the Vengeance. But there were hard times in between, most notably Tacker losing his fiancée in a plane crash while he was piloting. If anyone had reason to spin out of control, ending up driving drunk and crashing his truck, it was him.

Luckily, that's behind him. He battled through it with the help of counseling and falling in love with Nora. While there's no wedding planned for them yet, I expect it's just a matter of time.

Speaking of weddings, I glance around the table. "Are all of you going to Erik and Blue's wedding tomorrow?"

I get four nods in return, which is what I expected, but I wasn't quite sure. Tomorrow's nuptials were thrown together spontaneously after the season concluded. Turns outs, when a surprise baby happens along, people need to adjust their plans. Erik and Blue traded in a big fancy wedding for a get-together at their house with just the team and close family. Erik is renowned for his parties, and there will be food, cake, and music, promising a fantastic time for all.

"Want to come back here tomorrow?" Jett asks the group. "After all the frivolity dies down? We can probably steal the Cup right out from under Erik's nose, then bring it here with us."

We all laugh at the thought. It's tradition that each player of the team is allowed twenty-four hours with the Cup, and Erik's going to have it at his place tomorrow for the wedding. But there's no way in hell it will get snatched out from under his nose as that Cup travels with an attendant who will never let it out of his sight.

Jim shakes his head. "I'm out. I have Lucy for the weekend, so we'll be hanging out together or she'll be locked in her room refusing to talk."

I wince. Jim's had it tough since separating from his wife, Ella. It's been bitter with a lot of recrimination on both sides, and their daughter, Lucy, has not been making it easy on Jim, seemingly laying the blame on his doorstep. I truly don't know what's happened between the two, but I know Jim's been struggling with it all.

"I'm in," Baden replies to Jett's invitation for another Sneaky Saguaro night out.

Kane nods. "Me too."

All eyes come to me, everyone expecting me to throw my hat in the ring. After all, I'm *the* most notorious playboy on the team. There's a reason everyone calls me Wylde instead of my first name, Aaron.

"I'm out," I reply, smirking at the shocked faces staring back at me.

"Got a date," I tell them, purposely leaving the vague words hanging.

I get nothing but blank expressions.

"You know… man takes woman out?" I tease.

"No, seriously," Kane says, shaking his head. "There has to be some other reason. Aaron Wylde does not date."

The resounding laugh comes from deep within my belly. What he said was usually true. Asking the hot nerdy bookstore owner out was definitely uncharacteristic of me, so I feed them a bit more. "She's my date to the wedding tomorrow."

Kane looks to Jett. "We can bring dates to weddings?"

Jett shrugs as if this is a foreign concept. "Maybe in this country, you can, but in Sweden… never heard of this."

There's more laughter, but Jim is the one who presses me. "You're bringing a date to the wedding? Is it serious?"

My chin pulls inward, my eyes round with faux horror. "No, it's not serious. Just met her yesterday, as a matter of fact. She owns a bookstore downtown, and I wandered in—"

"You wandered into a bookstore?" Baden gasps outrageously. Wildly, he looks around the table. "Dudes… I fear Aaron Wylde has been kidnapped by aliens, and they currently possess his body."

Chuckling, I aim a sly wink his way. "Trust me... if you'd seen this woman, you would have wandered in, too."

"Smokin' hot?" Baden guesses.

"I wouldn't say smokin'," I hedge, thinking about her striking features.

"Big tits?" Jett asks.

I shrug. "Couldn't tell. Her shirt was too baggy."

Frowning, Jett looks to Jim for perhaps some explanation as to my weirdness. Jim just shrugs helplessly.

"Let's just say," I drawl, resting my forearms on the table, "that she pushed some of my buttons, and, if all goes well, the wedding and reception will then turn into an all-night event back at my place."

Kane slaps me on the back, pride on his face. "There's the Wylde we all know and love."

"I don't know," Jett drawls, staring pensively. "I think you're losing it. Not going to be the team playboy anymore. I mean... who picks up someone in a bookstore for a hookup?"

I lift my chin, giving him a cocky smirk. "I'll always be the team playboy."

"Prove it," Jett challenges, giving a long slow scan of the place. "Plenty of ladies in here right now. Make a move."

I'm enjoying the ribbing. It's half the fun of hanging

out with my mates. "Hey." I hold my arms out, trying for innocent. "I'm just enjoying my time with my buds, but the night is still young."

They make scoffing sounds, shaking their heads. Not buying it at all. And I simply can't have my reputation diluted by inaction, so I peruse the surrounding tables.

And right there.

Hot blonde with her friends, watching our table… clearly knowing who we are. When she locks eyes with me, I crook my finger, summoning her to my table. Her friends giggle, pushing her playfully out of her chair, and she rises. Tugging on her short skirt, she wobbles my way on ridiculously high heels and all the guys at my table start hooting at my bold move.

"He still has it," Kane says confidently, just low enough I can hear it.

"Hi," the blonde breathlessly says as she wedges her way in between Baden and me.

"Hi, yourself," I reply, checking her out. She's exactly my type, or, at least, the kind I preferred before a nerdy redhead caught my eye yesterday.

Regardless… it doesn't mean I can't appreciate a blonde tonight.

I open my mouth, getting ready to offer to buy her a drink, when my phone buzzes on the table before me, the screen lighting up.